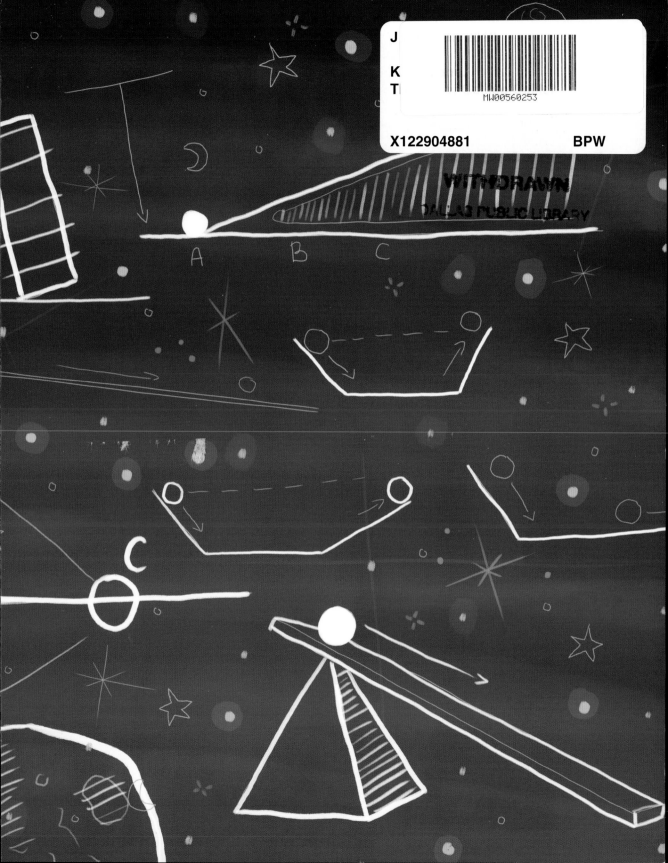

Illustrations by Isabel Muñoz.

Written by Jane Kent.

Designed by Nick Ackland.

WHITE STAR KIDS

White Star Kids® is a registered trademark property of White Star s.r.l.

© 2018 White Star s.r.l.
Piazzale Luigi Cadorna, 6
20123 Milan, Italy
www.whitestar.it

Produced by i am a bookworm.

ISBN 978-88-544-1335-1
    3 4 5 6   24 23 22 21 20

Printed in Turkey

The life of Galileo Galilei

WSKids
WHITE STAR KIDS

My name is Galileo Galilei, and I am an astronomer, physicist and philosopher.

Sometimes I am referred to as "The Father of Modern Science", because my work has had long-lasting implications in the area of physics.

Join me on my pioneering journey, as I make observations about nature and then use mathematics to prove them.

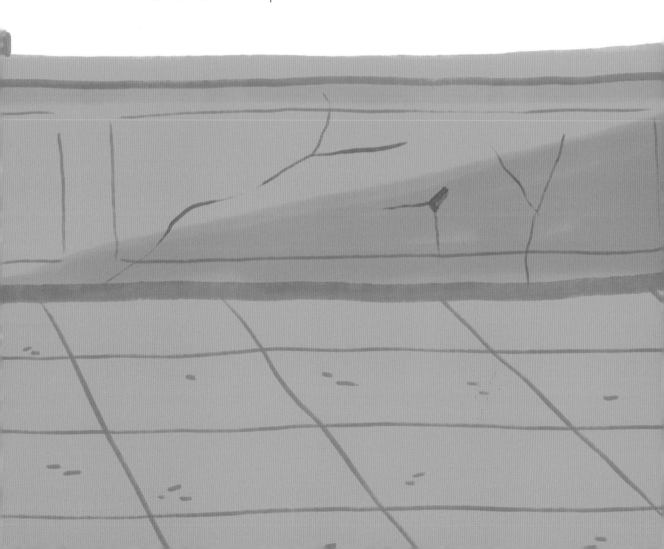

On 15th February, 1564, I was born in Pisa, Italy. My mother was Giulia Ammannati and my father was Vincenzo Galilei, a well-known musician and music theorist. I was the eldest of seven children born to them.

Vincenzo Galilei

Giulia Ammannati

Galileo Galilei

In 1574, my family moved to Florence and I began my formal education at the Camaldolese Monastery in Vallombrosa.

Whilst at the monastery, I thought about becoming a monk. However, my father had other ideas, and in 1580 he sent me to the University of Pisa to study medicine.

I was fascinated by many subjects, but philosophy and mathematics especially and so I changed my degree. I learned all about the Aristotelian view of the world, which was the scientific authority then - and the only one permitted by the Roman Catholic Church.

In 1585 I began a two-decade-long study on objects in motion. I published the first results in 1586 in a text called "The Little Balance," where I suggested an accurate method to weigh objects in air and water using a balance. My work made me a little famous.

This fame helped me to get a job as professor of mathematics at the University of Pisa in 1589. Whilst there I conducted experiments with falling objects and then wrote a text called "On Motion".

My conclusions about motion and falling objects moved away from the traditional Aristotelian view, and this angered some of my colleagues. Sadly, when my contract with the university expired in 1592, it was not renewed.

Thankfully I quickly found another professor of mathematics role, this time at the University of Padua. I stayed there for 18 years and during that time I conducted a variety of experiments and gave entertaining lectures that attracted large crowds.

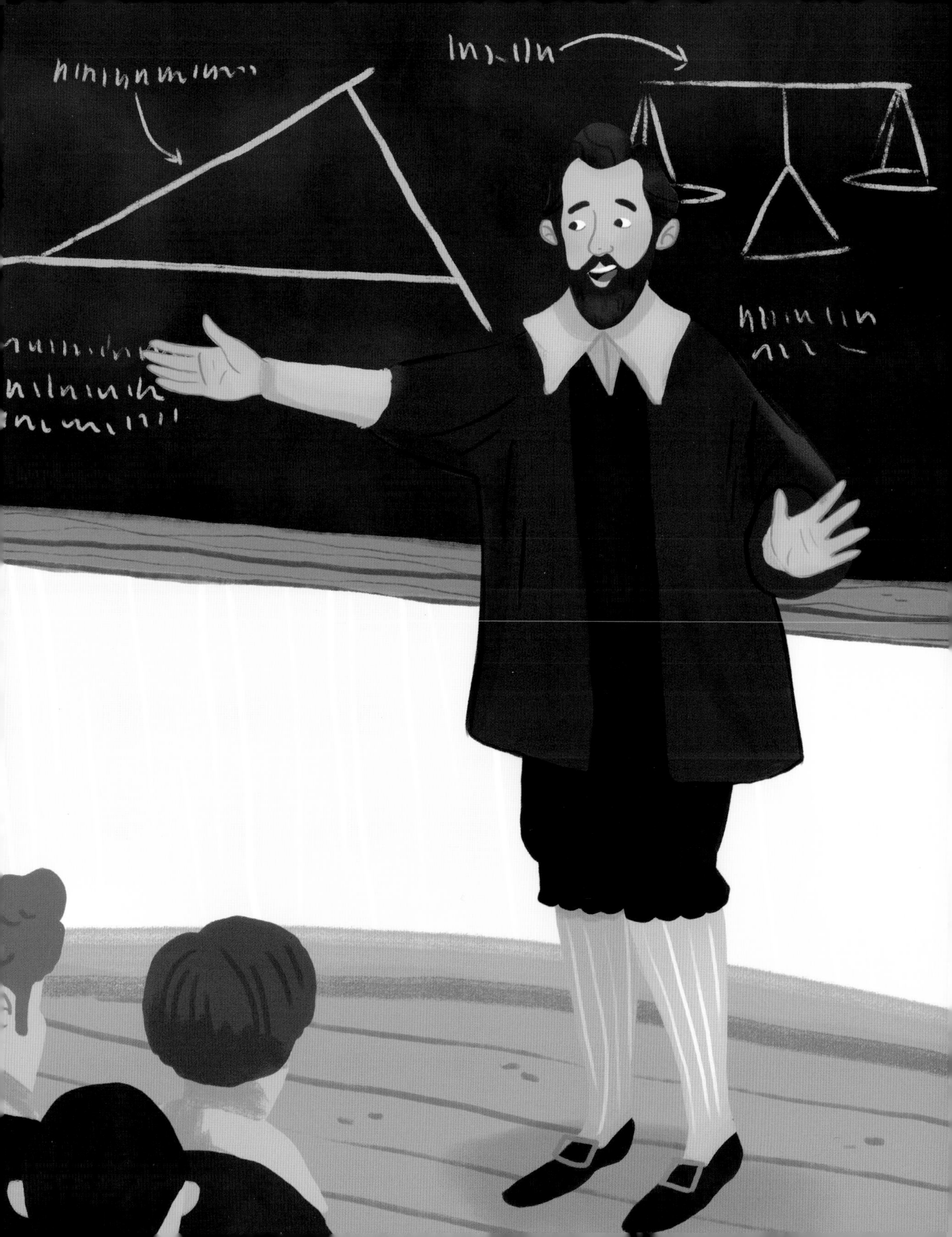

In 1600, I met Marina Gamba, a Venetian lady. Although we never married, we had three children together. Our two daughters were called Virginia and Livia and our son was called Vincenzio.

Virginia

Livia

Vincenzio

Marina
Gamba

In July 1609, I heard some intriguing news about the invention of a telescope by some eyeglass makers in Holland. I immediately decided to construct my own, and by August of that year I had completed the project.

When I demonstrated it to some Venetian merchants they realized it could be used to spot ships, and so they paid me to make several more for them.

I also found a different use for my telescope - to explore the universe. By pointing it towards the sky, I was able to make some incredible astronomical discoveries. I realized that rather than being flat and smooth, the moon was actually a sphere with mountains and craters on the surface. I also saw sunspots and observed that Venus has phases like the Moon, which proved that it rotated around the Sun.

Evidence that I collected using my telescope backed the Copernican theory - also known as the heliocentric view - which said that the Sun is really the center of the Universe and Earth and planets revolve around it. This theory was developed by Nicolaus Copernicus and published in 1543.

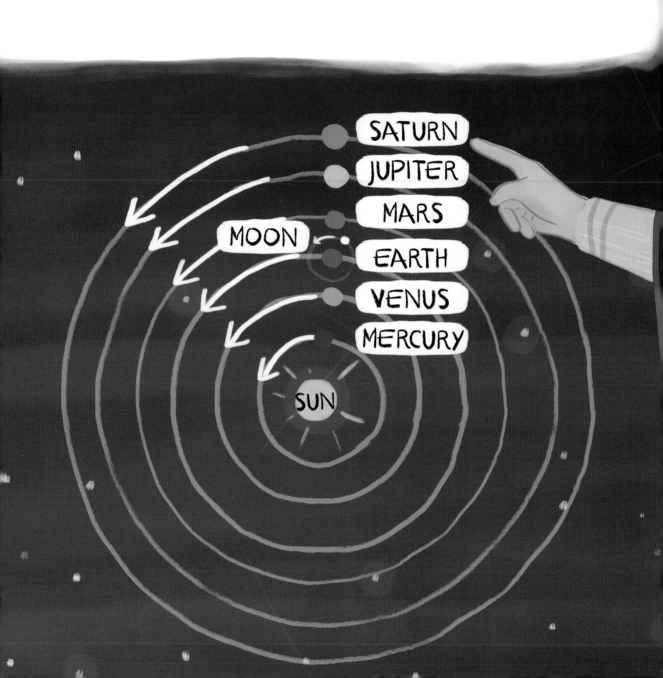

By supporting the Copernican theory rather than the Aristotelian one, which had been the Roman Catholic Church's philosophy since the Middle Ages, I was seen as going against the Catholic Church.

Members of the Church's Inquisition team declared the Copernican theory to be heretical and in 1616 they ordered me not to teach or defend it.

Seven years later my friend Cardinal Maffeo Barberini was elected to be Pope Urban VIII in 1623. With his blessing I was allowed to continue my astronomy studies and, as long as I was objective and didn't push the Copernican theory. Unfortunately, when my "Dialogue Concerning the Two Chief World Systems" text came out in 1632, it was viewed as advocating the theory and I was again condemned for heresy.

I was immediately called to Rome to appear before the Inquisition once more. Thankfully I wasn't imprisoned during the proceedings, as the case lasted from September 1632 until June 1633.

When the judgment finally came in, I was convicted of heresy and sentenced to life in prison. However, this was later reduced to house arrest and I was allowed to return to my villa at Arcetri, near Florence.

Whilst serving my sentence at home I continued to write. I published a text on my ideas on motion and mechanics called "Two New Sciences" in Holland in 1638.

My health began to decline and started going blind. On the 8th January 1642, I died at home in Arcetri at the age of 77.

Eventually, in 1757, the Catholic Church accepted that it could not longer deny the truth of the science and lifted the ban on most works supporting the Copernican theory.

Throughout the 20th century, many popes acknowledged my work, and in 1992 Pope John Paul II publicly declared that my findings had been correct all along. My contribution to science was finally accepted.

During my life I came to hold views that differed from the established views. It is important to be brave and stand strong in your own opinions, and never stop looking for evidence to back them up. But equally, you should always be prepared to listen to the ideas of others - after all, you never know what you might learn from them!

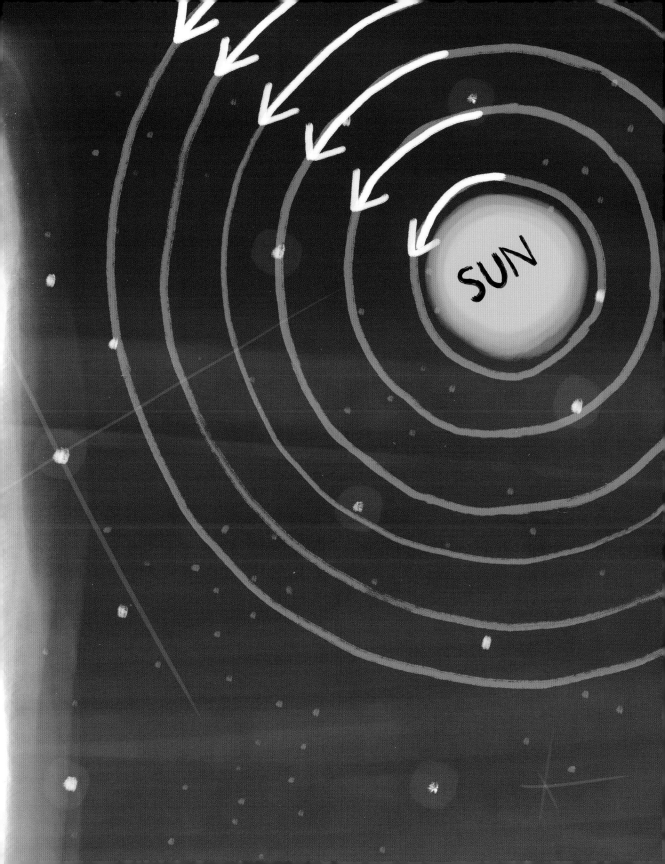

Galileo Galilei
was born on 15th
February in Pisa,
Italy.

He studies at
the University
of Pisa and first
learns about the
Aristotelian theory.

1564

1583

1574

1585

The Galilei family
moved to Florence
and Galileo began
studying at the
Monastery in
Vallombrosa.

ITALY

Galileo leaves university without
completing his degree. He begins studying
objects in motion.

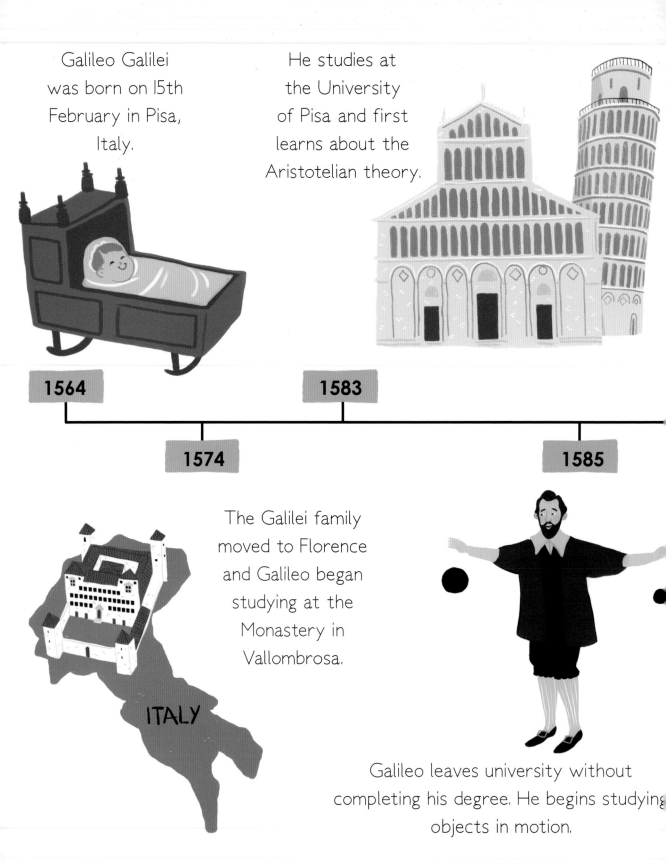

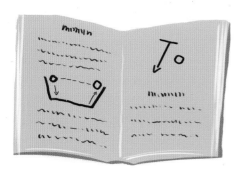

Galileo writes "On Motion," which moves away from the Aristotelian view and angers his colleagues.

He meets Marina Gamba and they go on to have three children together.

1589

1600

1592

1609

Galileo creates his own telescope to explore the Universe and make incredible astronomical discoveries.

He becomes professor of mathematics at the University of Padua.

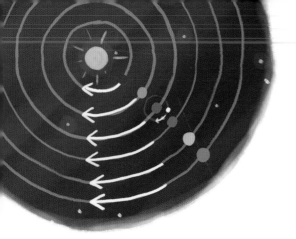

Galileo's studies support the Copernican theory. He is ordered by the Church not to teach or defend it.

He is called to Rome to appear before the Inquisition again.

1616

1632

1623

1633

Cardinal Maffeo Barberini is elected to be Pope Urban VIII. He allows Galileo to continue his astronomy studies.

He is found guilty and spends the rest of his life under house arrest at his villa at Arcetri.

Galileo publishes his ideas on motion and mechanics in "Two New Sciences" in Holland.

The ban on most works supporting the Copernican theory is lifted by the Catholic Church.

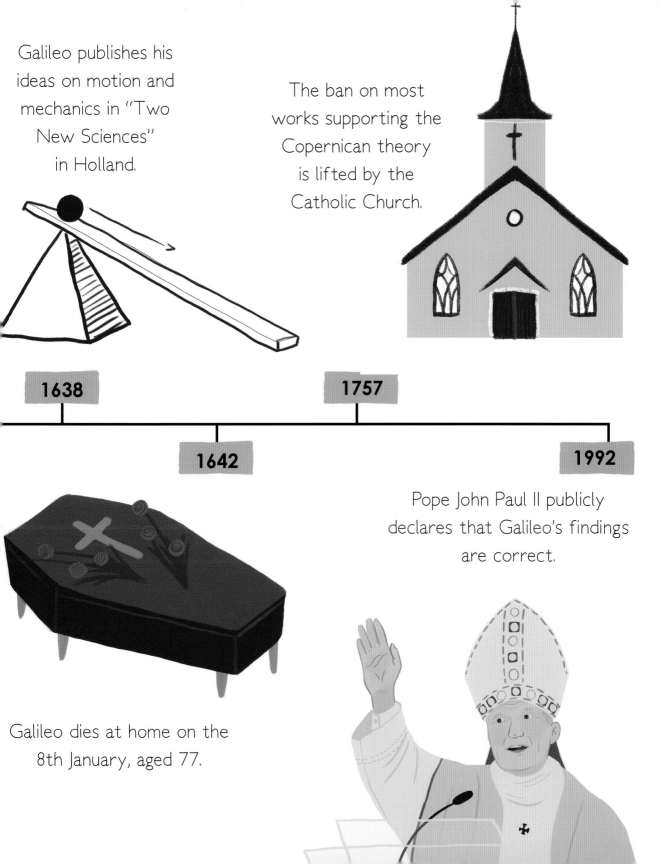

1638

1757

1642

1992

Pope John Paul II publicly declares that Galileo's findings are correct.

Galileo dies at home on the 8th January, aged 77.

QUESTIONS

Q1. Galileo was the eldest
of how many children?

Q2. Where did Galileo first learn about
the Aristotelian theory?

Q3. How many years did Galileo stay
at the University of Padua?

Q4. What were the names of Galileo and Marina
Gamba's children?

Q5. In what year did Galileo make his telescope?

Q6. What did observing that Venus has phases like the moon prove?

Q7. In 1616 the Roman Catholic Church banned Galileo from teaching what theory?

Q8. Which of Galileo's friends was elected to be Pope Urban VIII?

Q9. What was Galileo's sentence of life in prison late reduced to?

Q10. When was the ban on most works supporting the Copernican theory lifted by the Catholic Church?

DIS

DIMOS

MATE

intorno a

MECANICA & N

GALILEO C

Filofofo e Matern

Grau

ANSWERS

A1. 7.

A2. The University of Pisa.

A3. 18.

A4. Virginia, Livia and Vincenzio.

A5. 1609.

A6. That it rotates around the Sun.

A7. The Copernican theory.

A8. Cardinal Maffeo Barberini.

A9. House arrest.

A10. 1757.